The King and I

Written and Illustrated by
Sorel Kairé

MW00905650

Copyright © 2019 Sorel Kairé.

All rights reserved. No part of this book may be reproduced, stored, or transmitted by any means—whether auditory, graphic, mechanical, or electronic—without written permission of the author, except in the case of brief excerpts used in critical articles and reviews. Unauthorized reproduction of any part of this work is illegal and is punishable by law.

ISBN: 978-1-6847-0297-8 (sc)
ISBN: 978-1-6847-0296-1 (hc)
ISBN: 978-1-6847-0295-4 (e)

Library of Congress Control Number: 2019907139

Because of the dynamic nature of the Internet, any web addresses or links contained in this book may have changed since publication and may no longer be valid. The views expressed in this work are solely those of the author and do not necessarily reflect the views of the publisher, and the publisher hereby disclaims any responsibility for them.

This is a work of fiction. All of the characters, names, incidents, organizations, and dialogue in this novel are either the products of the author's imagination or are used fictitiously.

Lulu Publishing Services rev. date: 06/11/2019

Table of Contents

to:

from:

To my mother, Blanca, for gifting me this story. To my dad, Victor, for making it come true

The King And I
by
Sorel Kairé

THE KING AND I

"It's a girl," the midwife announced to the king, who was pacing the halls of his castle.

"It's a girl and the queen is finally resting."

The king stopped and breathed a sigh of relief. The queen had taken almost twenty-five hours to give birth to their baby, a very long time for a lady as frail and regal as his wife. He was happy she was well, but felt a wave of disappointment as he digested the three words uttered by the midwife.

It's a girl

He had been hoping for a boy.

The court's wise woman and seer of the future had told him many moons ago that he and his queen would have only one child.

"It's a girl," he heard again, the words became imprinted in his mind.

The king sighed.

Whom would he guide to be strong and wise? Whom would he teach to read and ride and sing and swim and row and fish and talk to the stars? To whom would he entrust his most important secrets? Who would continue to rule in his place?

Who? Who? Who?

The midwife spoke again and broke into his thoughts. "Your majesty, you may see them now. But be brief, the queen needs her sleep."

He turned and headed for their room. *A girl*, he thought, disillusioned.

He entered his chamber and heard the screams of his newborn child. He looked toward the hearth and spied the small crib. He sighed and turned his gaze to his queen.

She was resting on a cloud of pillows, her fragile face then paler than the silver glow of the moon. Her eyes were closed and her breathing was even. He smiled and brushed a tender kiss on her lips.

Oh, how he loved his queen.

The queen opened her eyes. A blush of excitement colored her cheeks when she saw her husband's beloved face.

"Have you seen her?" she whispered.

"No," he said and looked away, sad.

The queen smiled. She understood what her husband was feeling.

"I know you had your heart set on a boy to follow in your footsteps, but listen," she said.

"Listen?"

She motioned weakly towards the hearth. After a minute, the king frowned because he couldn't escape the sounds coming out of the crib.

"Listen to her voice. She is strong. She is bright. She will make you proud."

She's right, thought the king. *Her cries have strength and demand immediate attention.*

"She reminds me of someone I know," said the queen.

I'm hungry, I'm tired, I'm scared, the baby cried.

I am all alone!

Where is my mother's heartbeat? It made me feel safe and warm. Where is it? I can't hear it. I can't feel it. I'm cold. I'm hungry. I'm mad and all I can hear is the sound of my screams. They scare me. The more I cry, the more I can't stop. She shivered.

I am so afraid.

She felt a soft wind brush away her tears. Holding her breath, she decided to be brave and open her eyes. To her surprise, she found a big, straight, noble nose pointing directly at her face, two round nostrils blowing warm air in her direction. She forgot about her crying and, instinctively, her hands reached up.

Strong grip, thought the king as he felt the little fingers tighten firmly around his nose.

The girl let out a delighted scream and, at that precise moment, they saw each other. A strong current went through the king's body as he looked into his daughter's eyes for the first time.

It was love at first sight!

Father and daughter both felt it. This was a bond, strong and special. The king had found his princess and the girl had met her hero.

The king touched her nose with his index finger. She smiled.
"So soft," he whispered.

So gentle, she thought.

The king let his finger run down her face and arm until he found the baby's tiny hand. She gripped his finger with a force that surprised him.

I found the one that I'll teach to read, to play, to ride, to fish...

...to sing, to govern, to care for our people, to talk to the stars and to love, thought the king, his heart full of pride.

To love.

The king kissed his daughter's hand and carefully, very carefully, picked the baby girl up in his arms and hugged her to his chest for the very first time. She sighed happily and, within seconds, was fast asleep, rocked by the rhythmic sound of the beating of her father's heart.

the end

PHOTOS/DRAWINGS

21

AUTHOR'S NOTE

This story is about Love. Unconditional Love. Empowering Love. Looking at life through Love-Colored glasses makes the hard somehow turn soft. I am blessed to live in a world full of Love. Love... because I have all of you in my life.

Many, many people have made my life lovely. Thank you.

Mr. Thomas, my High School English teacher, was the first person that recognized I could write, even if I didn't get it.

My family... Manuel, Manuelito, Janina, Nadine, Juan Manuel, Jose Emilio, Diego, Fede and Javier. I feel your Love even when I am not with you.

My other family... Barbara, you are my Rock. Diego, Saveria and Rodrigo, children of my heart, for loving me unconditionally.

My LA Family... Tía Fortuna, Sandy and Randy for being there for me. Always.

My Soul Sisters... Ioanna, Regina, Stephanie, Astrid, Vivian, Lucy, Julia, and Carol for making my life better and sweeter.

My teacher, Toni Lopopolo, who taught me the rules, even though I broke all of them in this book.

And a very special thanks to Edgar, for recognizing my Girl Power, loving this story, and encouraging me to make it come to life.

AUTHOR'S BIO

Sorel Kairé was born and raised in Guatemala. She moved to Los Angeles to attend college, and has been living and working there ever since. Today she works as a script supervisor for sitcoms. Although Sorel has been telling stories her entire life, The King and I is her first book.